SHIELD UP!

TO MIKE, SUSIE, AND MY FRIENDS WITH LOVE AND GRATITUDE. *–MMC*

TO MY DAUGHTER, CHIARA. *—AP*

Published by
MAGINATION PRESS
An Educational Publishing Foundation Book
American Psychological Association
750 First Street, NE
Washington, DC 20002

For more information about our books, including a complete catalog, please write to us, call 1-800-374-2721, or visit our website at www.apa.org/pubs/magination.

Book design by Sandra Kimbell

Printed by Worzalla, Stevens Point, WI

Library of Congress Cataloging-in-Publication Data
Craver, Marcella Marino.
Shield up! : how upstanding bystanders stop bullying / by Marcella Marino Craver, MSEd, CAS ; illustrated by Amerigo Pinelli.
pages cm
ISBN-13: 978-1-4338-1651-2 (pbk.)
ISBN-10: 1-4338-1651-2 (pbk.)
1. Bullying in schools—Comic books, strips, etc.—Juvenile literature 2. Bullying—Prevention—Comic books, strips, etc.—Juvenile literature 3. Graphic novels. I. Pinelli, Amerigo, illustrator. II. Title.
LB3013.3.C73 2015
371.7'82—dc23
2013048065

Manufactured in the United States of America
First printing March 2014
10 9 8 7 6 5 4 3 2 1

BY MARCELLA MARINO CRAVER, MSED, CAS

ILLUSTRATED BY AMERIGO PINELLI

Magination Press • Washington, DC
American Psychological Association

DEAR READER,

Imagine you notice one kid picking on another in the cafeteria. The mean words the first kid hurls make you feel uncomfortable, so you:

A. Walk away; it's none of your business.

B. Watch and maybe laugh along—hey, you don't want to get picked on too.

C. Say something to the kid who's acting mean; you've got this.

D. Get an adult.

E. All of the above.

Unfortunately, imagining this is possible because everyone has been a bystander. No one likes to watch or receive unkind treatment; and most people don't like to act mean—yet it happens daily! Life would be better if people didn't mistreat others, but few of us realize we possess the power to reduce these situations.

Have you received a compliment, a favor, or an unexpected smile from someone that momentarily improved your life? Have you seen a bystander stand up, shielding someone from unkind acts? Kind behavior uplifts all of us. Think of one small, kind action as a pebble tossed in a still lake. When the pebble breaks the water's quiet surface, concentric circles form and span well beyond the pebble's impact. Give it a try. Like a pebble, your kind act will not only affect the person who directly received it, but it will impact those around you because kindness is contagious.

So what's your answer?

Shield Up! tells the story of friends who choose to do **E:** All of the above. At first they laugh along with their friend's mean behavior until they realize that laughing and ignoring her nastiness make it worse. It's not easy, but they stand up to her even though it risks their friendship. (For more information on how they do it, refer to the Note to Readers section.)

If we try to act as upstanding bystanders shielding others from cruelty while practicing kindness, then we will transform every environment we enter, just like the pebble. Are you ready to *Shield Up?*

—*Marcella*

HEY, RYAN! TODAY'S THE DAY WE FIND OUT! I HOPE I GET A GOOD PART, AND YOU GET TO DESIGN THE COSTUMES.
I CAN'T WAIT TO GET TO SCHOOL AND SEE THE CAST LIST. I REALLY HOPE YOU, CJ, AND ZOE GET A PART!
WE BETTER HOPE CJ GETS DOROTHY.
YOU KNOW SHE WILL! SHE IS PERFECT IN EVERY WAY FOR IT.
I KNOW YOU'LL GET DOROTHY.
THANKS, ZOE. I HOPE ALL THREE OF US GET A PART.
THERE'S ZOE AND CJ! C'MON!
I HOPE CJ LIKES MY COSTUME IDEAS.

WHY SO QUIET, EVA?
I NEED TO GET A PART.
WHY?
MY OLD SCHOOL DIDN'T HAVE THEATER SO I WANT TO GIVE IT A TRY. PLUS, MAYBE I'LL MEET NEW PEOPLE.
YEAH, I REMEMBER WHEN I WAS THE NEW KID.
LET'S GO LOOK!

8TH GRADE
WIZARD OF OZ CASTING LIST
CJ: DOROTHY
JAX: TINMAN

8TH GRADE
WIZARD OF OZ CASTING LIST

CJ: DOROTHY
JAX: TINMAN
ZOE: SCARECROW
EVA: COWARDLY LION
ART: OZ
KED WITCH

LET'S ALL LOOK AT THE SAME TIME.
1...2...3...LOOK!

JAX! ZOE! WE'LL BE THE BEST IN THE SHOW! BETTER THAN THE NEW GIRL, ANYWAY, SHE'S AWFUL!

IT'S OKAY, MAYBE YOU'LL MAKE IT NEXT YEAR.
HEY, DON'T BLAME THE MESSENGER, BUT YOU DIDN'T GET A PART BECAUSE YOU SING LIKE A DYING CAT!

EVA, DID YOU BRIBE SOMEBODY TO GET YOUR ROLE?

GOOD JOB, CJ.
CONGRATULATIONS!
YOU DESERVE THE PART!
WAY TO GO!
YOU'LL BE GREAT!
NICE!
THANKS, ART! CONGRATS TO YOU! SEE YOU AT REHEARSAL!
-OZ-
Script
I CAN'T THANK YOU ENOUGH, MR. PALSON. I AM REALLY, REALLY ECSTATIC!

WELCOME! I'M MR. PALSON, THE DIRECTOR. THE CAST AND CREW SITTING AROUND YOU ARE YOUR NEWEST FAMILY. WE HAVE A SHOW TO DO AND THE ONLY WAY TO GET IT DONE IS TEAMWORK!
IS THIS SEAT TAKEN?
THE LOSERS SIT IN THE BACK.

TOMORROW MORNING, WE'LL MEET BEFORE SCHOOL FOR A READ THROUGH. PLEASE READ OVER THE SCRIPT TONIGHT TO GET FAMILIAR WITH IT.
NOT TO BASH HER, BUT HOW DID SHE GET A PART? I DON'T KNOW HOW THEY DID THINGS AT HER OLD SCHOOL, BUT HERE, YOU HAVE TO ACTUALLY BE ABLE TO READ THE SCRIPT.

AT MORNING REHEARSAL…
NICE FIRST READ THROUGH! NOW, LET'S WORK ON THE TONE TO MAKE IT SOUND MORE REALISTIC, LIKE EVA DID TODAY.

OZ

CJ, WHY ARE YOU IN EVA'S LOCKER?
THIS CAN'T BE GOOD.
SHHHH. WATCH THIS.

Wizard of
-OZ-
Script
BULLYING
BEHAVING IN A
mean WAY
one TIME
OR many TIMES,
on purpose,
TO SOMEONE
WHO MAY B
perceived TO
BE DIFFERENT
TA DA!!
GOT IT.
GOLDEN RULE:
TREAT OTHERS HOW
YOU
WANT TO BE TREATED
Wizard of
-OZ-
WHY IS SHE
DOING THIS?

THE NEXT DAY...
WHAT ARE SOME OF THE WAYS WE MIGHT ACT MEAN TO OTHERS?
WE CAN SAY MEAN THINGS.
YES. WHAT ELSE?
PHYSICALLY HURTING ANOTHER PERSON.
YES, THAT MAY LEAVE A BRUISE. WHAT DOES SAYING SOMETHING MEAN DO?

IT CAN LEAVE YOU FEELING BAD ABOUT YOURSELF OR LESS CONFIDENT.
BULLYING:
1. Behaving in a mean way.
2. One time or many times.
3. On purpose.
4. To someone who may be perceived to be different.
YES, WORDS OFTEN HURT FOR A LONGER TIME THAN A BRUISE. IT'S TOO BAD, BUT YOU CAN'T TAKE BACK HURTFUL WORDS SO LET'S TRY TO SAY POSITIVE THINGS TO LIFT EACH OTHER UP! HOW ELSE CAN WE BE MEAN TO OTHERS?

CYBERBULLYING?
YES, USING THE INTERNET OR A PHONE TO HURT SOMEONE IS VERY SERIOUS. WHAT ABOUT EXCLUDING SOMEONE ON PURPOSE?
THAT HAPPENED TO ME IN FOURTH GRADE. I DIDN'T GET WHY SUDDENLY MY FRIENDS WERE NOT MY FRIENDS ANYMORE. THEY JUST LEFT ME OUT. IT MADE ME HATE SCHOOL!
I BET IT TOOK SOME COURAGE ON YOUR PART TO COME TO SCHOOL AND FIND A NEW GROUP OF FRIENDS. UNFORTUNATELY, WHEN PEOPLE BULLY, THEY AREN'T THINKING ABOUT THE OTHER PERSON'S FEELINGS.
STORY

BULLYING:
1. Behaving in
2. One time or many times.
On purpose.
To someone who may
be perceived to be different.
younger
I DON'T GET NUMBER 4. AREN'T WE ALL PRETTY MUCH THE SAME?
THE PERSON WHO IS BULLIED MAY BE SINGLED OUT FOR A NUMBER OF REASONS. IT MAY BE SOMEONE WHO IS YOUNGER, FOR EXAMPLE; OR SOMEONE WHO IS LESS SECURE; WHO LOOKS OR ACTS DIFFERENTLY; WHO IS ALONE; WHO YOU THINK YOU ARE BETTER THAN; OR WHO HAS A DISABILITY.

ANOTHER IMPORTANT POINT IS THAT THERE IS OFTEN AN IMBALANCE OF POWER. THE BULLIED PERSON MAY HAVE TROUBLE DEFENDING HIMSELF OR HERSELF.

1. AN AGE OR STRENGTH DIFFERENCE

2. A SOCIAL STATUS DIFFERENCE
THE PERCEIVED IMBALANCE OF POWER CAN BE...

3. AN ABILITY DIFFERENCE

IF THE BULLYING CONTINUES, THE PERSON BEING BULLIED MAY FEEL EVEN MORE POWERLESS.

LATER THAT DAY...
SORRY I'M LATE, BUT I CAN'T FIND MY SCRIPT!
DON'T WORRY, WE'LL FIND MR. PALSON AND GET YOU A NEW COPY.
!!!
Wizard of -OZ-
WHERE DID YOU GET A NEW ONE?
MR. PALSON.
HOW DOES SHE KNOW THIS IS "A NEW ONE"? UNLESS SHE TOOK IT!

AFTER PLAY REHEARSAL...
STAGE ENTR
CJ, YOU READ PERFECTLY!
YOU WERE GREAT!
HOW DID EVA GET A SCRIPT!?

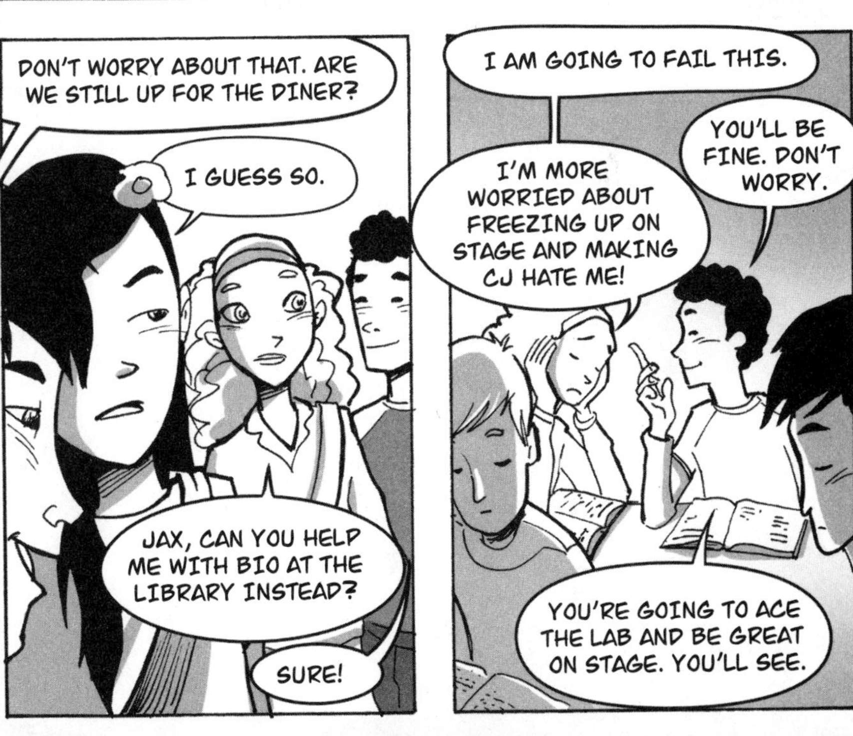
DON'T WORRY ABOUT THAT. ARE WE STILL UP FOR THE DINER?
I GUESS SO.
JAX, CAN YOU HELP ME WITH BIO AT THE LIBRARY INSTEAD?
SURE!
I AM GOING TO FAIL THIS.
YOU'LL BE FINE. DON'T WORRY.
I'M MORE WORRIED ABOUT FREEZING UP ON STAGE AND MAKING CJ HATE ME!
YOU'RE GOING TO ACE THE LAB AND BE GREAT ON STAGE. YOU'LL SEE.

AT THE DINER...

I STARTED TO SKETCH THE SETS AND COSTUMES. WHAT DO YOU THINK OF THIS?
IT LOOKS GREAT....DID YOU HEAR THAT EVA IS DATING THAT TROLL TODD IN SEVENTH GRADE!? I MEAN ICK!

AT EVA'S HOUSE...
ARE YOU DATING TODD?
NO!
I HEARD IT FR
MICHAELLA W
HEARD IT FRO
ALLIE WHO HE
IT FROM CJ A
THE DINER.

I DON'T FEEL GOOD, MOM. I DON'T WANT TO GO TO SCHOOL.
AGAIN? IS ANYTHING WRONG?
NO.
PLENTY. BUT CJ WILL BE WORSE IF I TELL!

IS EVA OUT AGAIN? THAT MAKES ONE FULL WEEK. HOPE SHE IS OK.
HOPE SHE AND TODD AREN'T FIGHTING.

AFTER CLASS...
CJ HAS SEEMED A BIT DIVA-FIED LATELY.
HUH?
YEAH. BUT I'VE BEEN AFRAID TO SAY ANYTHING TO HER ABOUT IT.
WHAT DO YOU MEAN? DO YOU THINK GETTING THE PART HAS GONE TO HER HEAD?
DUH?!?!? SHE'S BEEN ACTING SO MEAN, ESPECIALLY TO EVA.
MAYBE WE SHOULD SAY SOMETHING TO CJ ABOUT IT.
WHAT IF SHE GETS MAD AT US FOR SAYING SOMETHING?
WHAT IF IT MAKES IT WORSE FOR EVA?

WHAT'S UP WITH THE LOOKS?
EVA'S BEEN OUT FOR A WEEK.
SO? CALL ME A HATER, BUT I HOPE SHE IS WORKING ON HER LINES! IF NOT, SHE'LL RUIN THE SHOW FOR ALL OF US! AM I RIGHT?
I DON'T THINK SHE'S BAD AT ALL.
SERIOUSLY!? SHE'S A TRAINWRECK!
HEY, LET'S GET EVERYONE IN OZ TO STOP TALKING TO HER!
WHY?
WHY NOT? IT WILL BE FUN! GOTTA RUN...SEE YOU AT REHEARSAL!
OK, WE DEFINITELY HAVE TO DO SOMETHING!
MRS. SPIAGGA, CAN WE TALK TO YOU?
COME ON IN.
School Counselor

JAX, ZOE, AND RYAN EXPLAIN CJ'S BEHAVIORS TO MRS. SPIAGGA.
FIRST, BE PROUD OF YOURSELVES FOR COMING IN. THIS IS A VERY HARD THING TO TALK ABOUT. I'M HERE TO HELP YOU PROBLEM-SOLVE. WHAT DO YOU THINK YOU CAN DO?
MAYBE STAND UP TO HER?
BUT THAT WILL BE SOOOO HARD! SHE'S OUR FRIEND!
WHAT IF SHE GETS MAD AND TURNS AGAINST US?
LET'S TALK ABOUT ACTING AS UPSTANDING BYSTANDERS.
WHAT'S A BYSTANDER?
IN A BULLYING SITUATION, THERE IS THE PERSON BULLYING, THE PERSON BULLIED, AND THE BYSTANDER.
LOTS OF STUDENTS ARE BYSTANDERS. RIGHT?
YES! HAVE YOU ACTED TO STOP CJ'S BULLYING?

WHAT CAN WE DO? SHE'S BEEN OUR FRIEND SINCE 4TH GRADE!
WE COULD HAVE SPOKEN UP, AS A GROUP.
OR WE COULD HAVE TOLD MR. PALSON SOONER.

GOOD IDEAS! LET'S BRAINSTORM A FEW MORE.
MAYBE BRING AN ADULT TO HELP?
WE SHOULDN'T HAVE LAUGHED OR SMILED. THAT MAY HAVE ENCOURAGED CJ MORE!
I FEEL SO BAD FOR EVA. MAYBE WE SHOULD HAVE INCLUDED HER MORE, OR AT LEAST ASKED HER IF SHE WAS OK.
MAYBE WE COULD HAVE MADE AN EXCUSE TO GET EVA AWAY FROM CJ.

HERE'S A WAY TO REMEMBER THESE IDEAS!

S SPEAK UP TOGETHER

H HELP

I INCLUDE EVERYONE

E EXCUSE THE PERSON BEING BULLIED

L LEAVE TO TELL AN ADULT

D DO NOT WATCH

UP! UPLIFT EACH OTHER

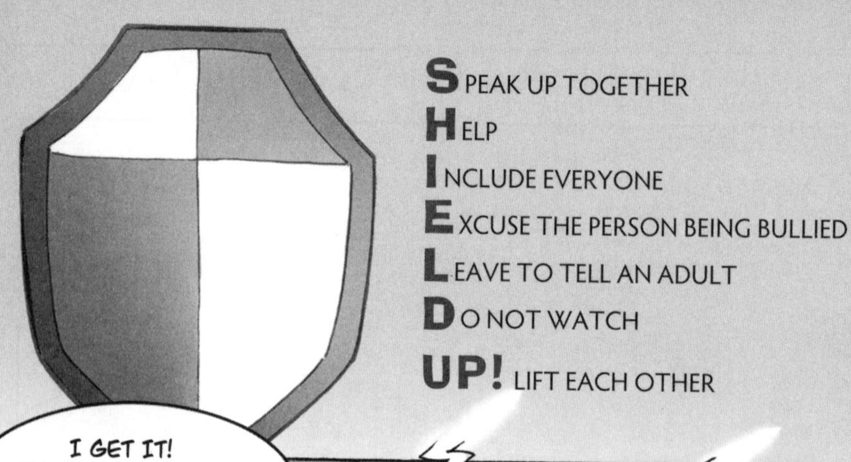
SPEAK UP TOGETHER
HELP
INCLUDE EVERYONE
EXCUSE THE PERSON BEING BULLIED
LEAVE TO TELL AN ADULT
DO NOT WATCH
UP! LIFT EACH OTHER

I GET IT! BYSTANDERS CAN BE A SHIELD AGAINST BULLYING! COOL!

YOU HAVE THE POWER TO IMPROVE THE SITUATION.

AT REHEARSAL, THE GANG PRACTICES BEING UPSTANDING BYSTANDERS.
ART, YOU NEED TO GET YOUR ACT TOGETHER...
HEY, LET'S GIVE ART A BREAK HERE.
HE'S DOING FINE!
THANKS, GUYS.

HEY! EVA'S BACK.
HI EVA. WELCOME BACK! HOW ARE YOU?
SIT HERE!

IT'S TWO WEEKS 'TIL OPENING NIGHT, AND WE NEED TO BE WORKING MORE LIKE A TEAM. LET'S SUPPORT EACH OTHER! THAT'S A WRAP FOR TODAY. GO HOME AND REST.

THE NEXT WEEK...
School Counselor
SHIELD UP
THANKS FOR AGREEING TO COME TO THIS GROUP. YOU'VE ALL RECENTLY EXPERIENCED BULLYING BEHAVIOR.

THE TREATMENT YOU'VE RECEIVED, THE BULLYING, IS NOT YOUR FAULT. YOU DID NOTHING TO DESERVE IT. EVERYONE HAS THE RIGHT TO FEEL SAFE IN SCHOOL.

LET'S AGREE TO KEEP WHAT WE SAY CONFIDENTIAL SO WE ALL FEEL COMFORTABLE TO SHARE.

WRITE DOWN HOW YOU FELT WHEN YOU WERE BULLIED, AND PUT THE CARDS IN THE JAR.

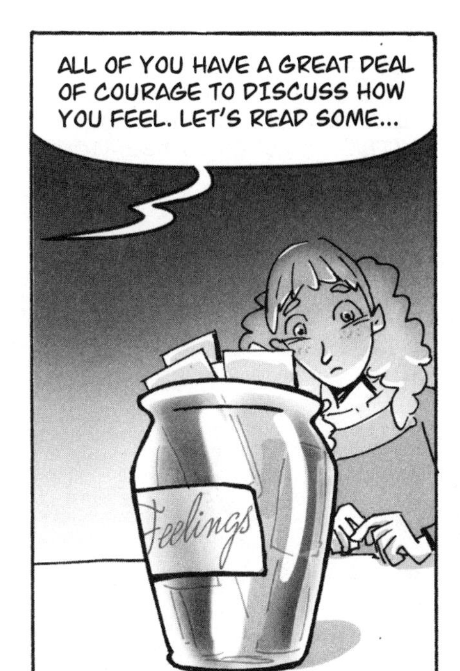
ALL OF YOU HAVE A GREAT DEAL OF COURAGE TO DISCUSS HOW YOU FEEL. LET'S READ SOME...
Feelings

I WAS JUST INFURIATED THAT MY SO-CALLED FRIENDS DID THIS! I TRUSTED THEM!

I HEAR ANGER, MISSY, AND BETRAYAL. ANYONE ELSE?

IT MADE ME WISH I WERE LIKE EVERYONE ELSE SO THEY'D STOP. BUT I'VE ALWAYS BEEN A LITTLE DIFFERENT. I USED TO BE PROUD OF BEING DIFFERENT.

MANY KIDS THINK THAT BLENDING IN WILL STOP THE BULLYING, BUT THAT DOESN'T WORK. INVOLVING AN ADULT OR FRIEND CAN HELP.

I FELT SO ALONE, SO ISOLATED. I DIDN'T WANT TO TELL ANYONE BECAUSE IT'S TOTALLY EMBARRASSING.

BULLYING CAN CREATE THAT FEELING OF ISOLATION. OR PEOPLE WHO BULLY MAY LOOK FOR THOSE WHO ARE ISOLATED. SO ALWAYS WALK WITH SOMEONE AND DON'T KEEP THE BULLYING TO YOURSELF.

LET'S ROLE PLAY SAYING "STOP!" IT MAY NOT BE EASY BUT "STOP!" WORKS BEST WHEN THE PERSON WHO IS BULLIED SAYS "STOP!" AND WALKS AWAY, PREFERABLY TO AN ADULT. BE AWARE THAT THE PERSON BULLYING MAY SEE "STOP!" AS A CHALLENGE, SO IT'S BEST TO TRY THIS STRATEGY WHEN OTHERS ARE AROUND.

STOP
STOP

POWERFUL POSTURE, DIRECT EYE CONTACT, AND A STRONG VOICE ARE IMPORTANT WHEN SAYING...
STOP
ANOTHER STRATEGY IS TO TRY TO MAKE LIGHT OF WHAT THEY ARE SAYING. YOU WANT TO LAUGH AT YOURSELF, NOT MAKE FUN OF THE PERSON DOING THE BULLYING. THIS IS NOT FOR EVERYONE, THOUGH, SO MAKE SURE YOU ARE COMFORTABLE WITH IT BEFORE YOU USE IT.

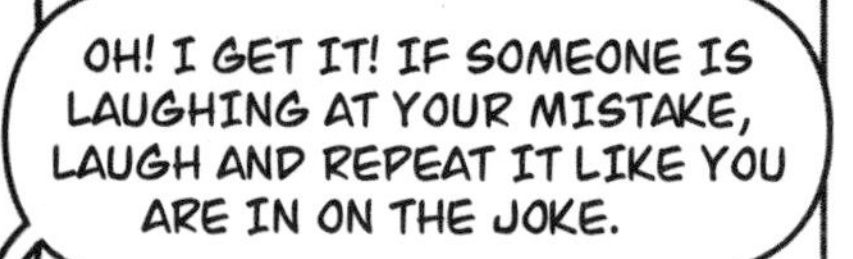

OH! I GET IT! IF SOMEONE IS LAUGHING AT YOUR MISTAKE, LAUGH AND REPEAT IT LIKE YOU ARE IN ON THE JOKE.
OR, IF SOMEONE MAKES FUN OF YOUR CLOTHES YOU CAN SAY "THANKS FOR THE FASHION ADVICE!" AND SMILE LIKE IT DOESN'T BOTHER YOU.

YES, IT'S BETTER THAN SHOWING FEAR, ANGER, OR SADNESS. YOU SHOULD STILL LEAVE QUICKLY AND REPORT THE INCIDENT TO AN ADULT IF YOU ARE UPSET BY IT.

YOU NEED TO FIND WAYS TO TAKE CARE OF YOURSELF AND COPE WITH THE STRESS.
YOGA CAN HELP, OR DOING SOMETHING YOU ENJOY, LIKE SPORTS OR DRAWING.
JUST TALKING ABOUT IT HAS MADE ME FEEL BETTER, BUT I ALSO LIKE PLAYING WITH MY CAT.

REMEMBER, BE WITH OTHERS; USE POWERFUL POSTURE, STEADY EYE CONTACT AND A CONFIDENT VOICE TO SAY "STOP"; OR USE HUMOR. TELL AN ADULT IMMEDIATELY. ALWAYS TAKE CARE OF YOURSELF!
THANKS!

AFTER SCHOOL...

EVA
THE STINKIEST SKUNK ON THE STAGE!
Tag: Zoe Jax Ryan Eva
LOL
:-)
HAHAHAHA!

AT REHEARSAL...
I HAVE SOME BAD NEWS. EVA HAS DECIDED NOT TO BE A PART OF OZ. I SPOKE TO HER MOTHER AND I AM SAD TO SAY THAT EVA ISN'T FEELING WELL ENOUGH FOR SCHOOL.
WE NEED TO SEE MRS. SPIAGGA AGAIN.
NOT SO CLOSE TO OPENING NIGHT!
POOR EVA.
WHAT ARE WE GOING TO DO?
THIS IS BECAUSE OF CJ, I KNOW IT!
LET'S TRY TO HAVE A PRODUCTIVE REHEARSAL TODAY. EVA'S UNDERSTUDY WILL TAKE OVER THE ROLE OF THE COWARDLY LION FOR NOW. OKAY, LET'S MOVE. PLACES FOR SCENE 7 IN 5!

ART! IF YOU COULD ONLY ACT YOU'D....
ART, I NEED YOU FOR ONE MORE COSTUME MEASUREMENT!
GOOD JOB, RYAN!
LET'S MEET AT MRS. SPIAGGA'S FIRST THING IN THE MORNING.
CJ NEEDS HER HELP!

CJ MEETS WITH MRS. SPIAGGA.
DO YOU KNOW WHAT THIS DEFINES?
1. Behaving in a mean way,
2. One time or many times,
3. On purpose,
4. To someone who may be perceived

BULLYING BEHAVIOR. YOU'VE BOTH RECENTLY BULLIED, AND IT MUST STOP. WE'LL WORK TOGETHER TO HELP YOU IMPROVE YOUR BEHAVIOR.

YES, CJ?
LIKE I TOLD THE PRINCIPAL, I DON'T THINK I BULLIED EVA. I WAS JUST KIDDING AROUND.

OKAY, LET'S NOT USE NAMES. LET'S EXAMINE YOUR BEHAVIOR AND DECIDE TOGETHER. WHAT HAPPENED?
1. Behaving in a mean way,
2. One time or many times,
3. On purpose,
4. To someone who
may be perceive
to be different.

BEHAVING IN A MEAN WAY
Wizard of -OZ- Script
I STOLE HER SCRIPT FROM HER LOCKER.
I MADE UP A RUMOR ABOUT HER.
EVA
THE STINKIES SKUNK ON THE STAGE!
AS A JOKE I PASTED HER HEAD ON A CUTE SKUNK PICTURE AND SENT IT TO OUR FRIENDS.

ONE TIME OR MANY TIMES
IT SOUNDS LIKE SHE DID STUFF TO HER OVER AND OVER, LIKE I DID TO A KID WHO I CAN'T NAME.
ON PURPOSE
DID YOU MEAN TO DO THOSE THINGS, ON PURPOSE?
I GUESS.

TO SOMEONE WHO MAY BE PERCEIVED TO BE DIFFERENT
HOW ABOUT NUMBER FOUR? TIM?
1. Behaving in a mean way,
2. One time or many times,
3. On purpose,
4. To someone who
I MADE FUN OF HIM BECAUSE HE STINKS AT SPORTS.
CJ?
SHE'S THE NEW GIRL.
DO YOU THINK YOUR RECENT BEHAVIOR FITS THE DEFINITION OF BULLYING?
YES.
THIS IS ABOUT YOUR BEHAVIOR, NOT WHO YOU ARE. YOU'VE MADE POOR CHOICES IN HOW YOU'VE ACTED. WE HAVE CONTROL OVER OUR BEHAVIOR. I THINK WE CAN AGREE, WE NEED TO MAKE BETTER CHOICES.

THIS MAY SOUND STUPID, BUT HOW SHOULD WE ACT?
THAT'S AN HONEST QUESTION. LET'S BRAINSTORM WAYS TO ACT KINDLY.

Think about others' feelings
Say nice things

Hang out with people who are alone

Only say NICE things about people who are not there

Say "I like your shirt"

Treat others the way you want to be treated

Tell a joke

Think about others' feelings

Say nice things

Say Please

Say thanks

Think before you act

Do a favor

Ask "How was your weekend?"

Avoid drama

Give a compliment

Include everyone

Do NOT repeat a rumor

Offer to lend a pen

Stand up for someone who is picked on

Talk about people's interests

Smile at people

LET'S THINK ABOUT HOW YOUR CHOICES HAVE AFFECTED OTHERS. TELL US A STORY OF SOMETHING YOU DID AND THEN LET'S IDENTIFY HOW THE OTHER PERSON FELT.
School Counselor
WELL, I MADE FUN OF HER FOR BEING THE NEW GIRL IN SCHOOL.
LET'S ATTACH SOME FEELINGS TO THAT, CJ.
I PROBABLY MADE HER FEEL INSECURE, I GUESS. SHE CAN'T HELP THAT SHE DOESN'T HAVE A LOT OF FRIENDS AT SCHOOL BECAUSE SHE'S NEW.
HOW DO YOU THINK IT FEELS TO BE MADE FUN OF FOR THINGS ABOUT YOURSELF YOU CAN'T HELP?
I KNOW HOW IT FEELS; IT FEELS AWFUL! IT MAKES YOU FEEL LIKE YOU WANT TO RUN AND HIDE!

IT SOUNDS LIKE THIS HAS HAPPENED TO YOU?
YEAH. IN THIRD GRADE EVERYONE CALLED ME TEENY, SHORTY, SQUIRT, A BUNCH OF MEAN NAMES. SO I WORE MY MOM'S SHOES TO SCHOOL TO BE TALLER AND EVERYONE LAUGHED EVEN HARDER. IT LASTED ALL YEAR. I STAYED HOME SICK A LOT.

IT FINALLY STOPPED WHEN I MET ZOE, RYAN, AND JAX. THEY DIDN'T CARE THAT I WAS SHORT.
I'M SORRY THAT HAPPENED TO YOU.
I'M SORRY I MADE HER QUIT OZ. HOW COULD SHE GET ON STAGE AFTER WHAT I SAID?
IT SOUNDS LIKE YOU ARE FEELING REMORSE.
I DIDN'T SEE HER SIDE. I WAS BEING JEALOUS, AND SELFISH TOO.
NOW YOU SEE HOW YOUR WORDS AND ACTIONS CAN AFFECT OTHERS. REMEMBER, THESE BEHAVIORS ARE CHOICES YOU'VE MADE, NOT WHO YOU ARE.

I KNOW WHAT I CAN DO TO HELP A LITTLE. I MEAN, I CAN'T UNDO EVERYTHING, BUT MAYBE I CAN FIX SOMETHING.
MR. PALSON?
COME IN.
I HAVE BEEN MAKING SOME REALLY BAD CHOICES LATELY... AND I KNOW WHY EVA QUIT.
'CAUSE I UPSET HER. CAN YOU GET HER TO COME BACK?
WHY?
I'M NOT SO SURE...
PLEASE TELL HER THAT CJ WON'T BE NASTY AGAIN. I PROMISE. I KNOW YOU WANTED US TO BE A FAMILY BUT I WAS TOO MUCH OF A DIVA TO LISTEN. BUT I GET IT NOW.
OK, I'LL TRY. BUT NO GUARANTEES.

AT REHEARSAL...
I THOUGHT THIS COULD HELP PROMOTE THE SHOW AND PROMOTE SOME GOOD WILL AROUND SCHOOL.
TICKETS?
OUR OZ FAMILY WILL WRITE ANONYMOUS, KIND MESSAGES ON THEM AND LEAVE THEM FOR OTHERS AROUND THE SCHOOL.
OZ
YOU JUST WRITE A COMPLIMENT OR NICE COMMENT FOR SOMEONE, LIKE "YOU ARE THOUGHTFUL," OR "NICE WORK AT PRACTICE," OR "YOU ARE A GREAT SINGER," AND LEAVE IT WHEN NO ONE WILL SEE YOU.
OZ
BY THE END OF THE WEEK...

SHE LOOKS SURPRISED.
HA HA, WOW. WAY TO FAIL.
HEY, NO WORRIES, YOU'LL DO BETTER NEXT TIME.
WE'RE STUDYING TOGETHER NEXT WEEK IF YOU WANT TO JOIN US.
Think about others' feelings
Say nice things
Say Please
Think before you act
Do a favor
Ask "How was your we
Avoid drama
Give
nclude everyone
Offer to lend a
Stand up for someone who
SORRY I LAUGHED.

AT DRESS REHEARSAL...
DON'T BE NERVOUS, ZOE. YOU'LL BE GREAT. IT'S ONLY A DRESS REHEARSAL.
WHAT IF I FORGET WHAT TO SAY?
JUST LOOK TO MR. PALSON BACKSTAGE; HE'LL FEED US LINES. DON'T WE LOOK AWESOME IN THESE COSTUMES RYAN DESIGNED? WE'LL HAVE TO TELL HIM LATER.
ZOE IS HAPPY!

AFTER SCHOOL...
MOM, MR. PALSON ASKED ME TO BE IN THE PLAY AGAIN. HE GUARANTEED THAT CJ WOULDN'T BE A PROBLEM FOR ME.
HOW DO YOU FEEL ABOUT THAT?
I'M NOT SURE. I REALLY WANT TO, BUT IT'S NOT WORTH THE DRAMA. I'M JUST STARTING TO FEEL BETTER ABOUT GOING TO SCHOOL.
IT'S REALLY UP TO YOU.
CJ AND I ARE ON STAGE TOGETHER A LOT...SO WHAT DO I SAY TO HER?
MAYBE YOU CAN ROLE PLAY THAT WITH MRS. SPIAGGA.
OK.
AT SCHOOL...
HAVE YOU MADE A DECISION?
BUY A TICKET, MRS. SPIAGGA—I'LL BE ON STAGE, UNDER THE LIGHTS!

CJ AND TIM DISCUSS THEIR PROGRESS WITH MRS. SPIAGGA.
HOW HAS IT FELT TO TREAT OTHERS WITH KINDNESS?
IT'S BEEN KINDA WEIRD, LIKE PEOPLE DON'T KNOW HOW TO ACT WITH ME.
FOR ME, IT'S LIKE MY FRIENDS SEEM MORE COMFORTABLE WITH ME. DOES THAT SOUND WEIRD?
WHAT YOU BOTH SAID MAKES SENSE. WHEN YOU BULLY, IT CREATES STRESS NOT JUST FOR THE TARGET BUT FOR THE BYSTANDERS AS WELL. SOMETIMES THE BYSTANDERS FEEL IT AS MUCH AS THE STUDENT WHO IS BULLIED.
I GUESS I HURT THE PEOPLE I CARE ABOUT MOST WHEN I ACTED THAT WAY.
IT SEEMS LIKE YOU'RE BOTH CHANGING YOUR BEHAVIORS FOR THE BETTER.
I THINK IT'S HELPED ME TO THINK ABOUT HOW OTHERS ARE FEELING. IT GUIDES MY ACTIONS A LITTLE BETTER.
ME TOO.

LATER, AT THE DINER...
I WANT TO SAY SORRY. AFTER TALKING TO MRS. SPIAGGA I REALIZED THAT HOW I ACTED TOWARD EVA AFFECTED ALL OF YOU TOO.
CJ, WE...
RYAN, WAIT. THIS IS REALLY HARD. I'M SORRY. THANKS FOR STILL STICKING WITH ME AND THANKS FOR TELLING MRS. SPIAGGA THAT I WAS OUT OF CONTROL.

WHAT'S THE TICKET SAY?
"YOUR COURAGE IS INSPIRATIONAL." I DON'T KNOW WHO GAVE IT TO ME BUT I REALLY LIKE IT.

AT REHEARSAL...
ATTENTION EVERYONE! I HAVE A SURPRISE...EVA WILL BE PART OF OUR PRODUCTION!

ARE WE OKAY?
NO. I AM SO SORRY, EVA. I KNOW I HURT YOU AND I WON'T BOTHER YOU ANY MORE. I PROMISE.
OK. WE WILL JUST ACT ON STAGE. NOTHING ELSE.
DEAL. LINES ONLY BETWEEN US. IS THAT OK, MR. PALSON?
SURE. I'LL BE NEARBY. JUST ASK IF YOU NEED HELP.

SCRIPT
EVA, IF YOU NEED HELP WITH MEMORIZING LINES, LET US KNOW.
THANKS!
IT'S GREAT THAT EVA IS BACK.
YEAH, OZ IS GONNA BE INCREDIBLE!
GLAD TO HAVE THE OLD CJ BACK, AS WELL.
WHAT?
THE DIVA HAS DISAPPEARED!
YOU WANT DIVA? CARRY MY BOOKS!
CARRY MINE, TOO!
NO WAY! EVEN IF YOU STEAL THE SHOW TOMORROW, I STILL WON'T CARRY THEM.

OPENING NIGHT
YOU WERE TERRIFIC, REALLY. I MEAN IT.
THANKS.

NOTE TO READERS

UNDERSTANDING BULLYING

It seems like you hear people talk about bullying more and more every day. "He's a bully." "CJ bullied her." "Sounds like a bully to me." Do we really know what it means? You might not always agree with your friends or get along with your classmates so when is it conflict and when is it bullying?

CJ didn't understand the difference until Mrs. Spiagga defined bullying. Then CJ realized her behavior fit the definition of "bullying," and she wanted to make things right with Eva. When keeping an eye on her own behavior, CJ made better choices about how she interacted with others, especially Eva. Like CJ, we've all behaved in ways we wish we could take back, whether it was something we regret doing or something we wish we had done.

WHAT IS BULLYING ANYWAY?

Let's break down the definition of bullying used in the book to understand it better:

Bullying is:

1. BEHAVING IN A MEAN WAY
2. ONE TIME OR MANY TIMES
3. ON PURPOSE
4. TO SOMEONE WHO MAY BE PERCEIVED TO BE DIFFERENT.

1. Behaving in a mean way: Sadly, there are many ways people choose to be mean. People use actions, words, and exclusion to act mean, and it can take place in person or online. Any of these behaviors cause more embarrassment if they happen in front of others. Physical mean behavior involves harmful contact such as a kick or a punch, or mean actions such as stealing. Since preschool, parents and teachers discouraged this behavior. They may have advised, "Use your words!" to encourage a more appropriate outlet for negative feelings. Physical acts often hurt others less than mean words, however, because the pain words inflict may last longer than the pain from a slap or pinch. The recipient may hear the nasty taunts repeatedly in his mind and the "sorry" he hears doesn't silence them. This includes any disrespectful language or act whether it happens in person or online. When someone is excluded—for example, by being left out or having others rally against him or her—it is less obvious, but no less painful. For example, a group's gossip about a girl they dislike causes her to be isolated. When CJ shooed Eva from the auditorium seats, she excluded her from the group.

2. One time or many times 3. On purpose: These parts of the definition need little explanation. The behavior can happen once or more than once and it is intentional. The person means to be mean. Even though CJ didn't know she bullied Eva, she did intend to be mean to her by taking her script and saying mean words.

4. To someone who may be perceived to be different: This part of the definition includes physical and behavioral differences and power imbalances. If someone makes fun of another because of something she can't change about herself or may find hard to change about herself (such as weight, religion, race, being new to school, etc.), that fits this part of the definition. This type of mean behavior creates an imbalance of power so that the person who is bullied may think she can't defend herself, or feel that she is less than the other person. The power imbalance has little to do with size or strength; it centers more on the person who is bullied and her view or perception of the relationship. Eva and CJ's power imbalance developed from Eva's lack of friends because she just moved to town. CJ's social status outranked Eva and provided CJ with the power in the interactions.

BULLYING VS. PEER CONFLICT

Situations that do not meet all of the above criteria are not considered bullying but are instead considered peer conflict. Peer conflict, or fighting with another person, means a disagreement or misunderstanding between two people who perceive they stand on equal ground. The conflict may stem from differing opinions or a joke gone bad and it may or may not be settled, but both people leave the argument with their dignity intact. The differences between the people have little or nothing to do with the reason for the conflict. For example, a person wearing glasses disagrees with a person who stutters about who will earn a place on the soccer team. Their differences don't play a part in their competition for the last spot on the team and neither feels a power imbalance. Feelings may be hurt purposefully while they throw insults but there are no feelings of powerlessness. While we might judge their behaviors as mean, it is unlikely to be bullying because neither of them brings their differences into the argument and both keep their power in the relationship.

THE ROLE OF BYSTANDERS

The good news? Most of us don't act as bullies. Most of us are bystanders: people who see the bullying happen. Watching these interactions creates uncomfortable and stressful feelings in bystanders who often feel sympathy for the person receiving the unkind treatment as well as worry that they may be the next target. Why is this *good* news? We as bystanders have the chance to change the negative situation we observe for the better. Our choices at that moment can make a difference in an interaction where someone feels isolated, humiliated, and hurt. We can help stop those feelings with actions that also remind the bully that everyone deserves to be treated with kindness and respect. How awesome is that? The power to transform...and we own it!

HOW BYSTANDERS CAN HELP

Now that you know what bullying looks like, you can step in, if you are comfortable, to stop it. That transforms us from bystanders to upstanding bystanders, ready to stop the mistreatment of others so no one will need to tolerate mean behavior again. No one pretends that this is easy, but if you choose to do something about bullying you'll not only be an upstanding bystander but also, depending on the circumstances, others might see you as a leader or even a hero.

HOW TO SHIELD UP!

You might find that some of the SHIELD UP! strategies feel more comfortable for you and those might be the ones you try first. You might want to practice the strategies before you use them, or plan with a friend about when to use them. Hopefully, remembering the words SHIELD UP! will help you remember the options you have when the situation arises.

S = SPEAK UP TOGETHER
H = HELP
I = INCLUDE EVERYONE
E = EXCUSE THE PERSON BEING BULLIED
L = LEAVE TO TELL AN ADULT
D = DO NOT WATCH
UP! = UPLIFT EACH OTHER

Speak up together: In a bullying situation, the person bullying doesn't expect anyone to speak up, so when two or more people do, it might be enough to rebalance the situation and take power away from the person who is choosing to act unkindly. This works best when bystanders plan ahead to speak up. Try to approach a peer who also sees the mistreatment and decide whether or not you should speak up. Maybe it is best to involve an adult because the situation seems intense or you think the person bullying will lash out at you. If you do decide to say something, you might decide to keep it short; a simple, "cut it out" or "give him a break" from the two of you may be enough to stop the action. Remember the tone of voice you use in this situation as well as your body language. Keep both strong: use a steady, meaningful tone of voice and a confident stance with arms crossed or hands on your hips. You want to sound and look like you mean what you say.

Help: When you decide to approach the person who received the mistreatment after it occurred, it sends a powerful message to him. It announces that you witnessed what happened and you care enough to try to help make it better, which helps him feel less isolated. Even if the mistreated person doesn't accept your help, at least your offer identifies you as an ally who doesn't ignore the mean behavior and that can be significant to someone who might feel negatively targeted. Your help can be a simple "Are you okay?" or an offer such as, "I can walk with you tomorrow, if you want." It can also be an action that makes right what just went wrong, such as collecting items that have fallen on the ground.

Include everyone: This kind action stops bullying in two ways:

1. It changes the environment to one of kindness and respect due to the contagiousness of kindness. This makes bullying stand out as more unacceptable.

2. Someone planning to mistreat another looks for isolated people to bully; therefore, the fewer isolated people there are, the fewer people to bully. Think for a minute of how it might feel to be alone in a class or at lunch. Day after day you watch as others laugh with friends or share stories while you sit silently, trying to disappear. You begin to dread entering that class or cafeteria and start to find reasons not to, and that makes it harder to go back in. The day you go back to the room, waiting to be isolated again, someone walks up to you and begins a chat that slowly erases that lonely feeling living inside of you. Maybe

the short discussion about the teacher or the food lasts only a minute but how did it feel to be acknowledged? Accepted? Included?

Excuse the person being bullied: A person being bullied wants to be anywhere but standing there getting bullied. Giving him an out grants him his wish. You'll need to pop in and out of the situation quickly and urgently. Encourage him to move away fast—this is highly important! You can announce that a teacher needs to talk to him, or that a game is starting up, or even that you yourself need help. Whatever you say, sound sure of yourself. There may be a taunt or two as you walk away but you will have successfully intervened and stopped a bad situation. He can't be bullied if he's not there!

Leave to tell an adult: You may choose to walk away from the situation quietly to find an adult, or announce that soon an adult will arrive, but either way involving an adult does stop bullying. If possible, take the person who is mistreated with you. You'll be using both the E and L of SHIELD! Some kids worry that bringing in adults will make the situation worse, but informed adults can closely watch kids interact, leaving the person who bullies with fewer opportunities. Remember, sometimes kids need reminders about acting kindly, respectfully, and fairly from adults to guide them into acting appropriately. Think of CJ: she didn't realize that she was bullying Eva. Only when Mrs. Spiagga pointed out her mistreatment did CJ understand that her behavior fit the definition of bullying.

Do not watch: Leave with the person who is bullied if you can! When you choose to stand by and watch bullying happen, you join the side of mistreatment. Why? By keeping quiet you signal acceptance of the poor behavior and give it strength because your inaction as a bystander increases the power imbalance against the person receiving the unkind behavior. Imagine you are the person being bullied: all those eyes watching and seeming to enjoy your embarrassment would create the feeling of an angry mob against you. Resolve to act as an upstanding bystander who refuses to watch it, refuses to support it, refuses to allow it, and rescues the mistreated person from it. If the person bullying hopes to gain status or attention from his actions then this spoils his plan and removes the motivation to act in this manner.

Uplift each other: If you want to act as an upstanding bystander, a great place to start is to uplift people all around you. Start with small actions that are easy and comfortable for you to do—for example, saying "thank you" or holding the door for a person behind you. Then try to increase the size and frequency of those deeds to one or more a day. Once you make it a habit, you'll realize that acting in a nice manner makes a difference. The rewards of behaving kindly will return to you over and over because kind acts make others feel good. Even those just witnessing your kind acts will feel good, and you'll feel good too! Once you start making others smile, you'll smile more too. Try to get your parent to smile by remembering to put your things away—it just might change their day. Do you say "please" and "thank you" regularly? Have you offered to help a peer with a jammed locker? What about that kid who can *never* find a pencil? Positive notes left on a desk (like Mr. Palson's tickets) work if you feel embarrassed about giving compliments face to face. Start a change in your circle of friends that might spread around the school. When a friend receives or witnesses your thoughtful acts, she will do the same for someone else.

Contagious kind acts change you, change others, and change the environment for the better. Remember that pebble that represented one kind act from the Dear Reader section? It broke the water's surface and changed the water at the point of entry but also beyond its physical reach as it formed bigger and bigger circles. Those circles represented how kind acts spark more kind acts in different people. Now imagine 20 pebbles tossed into a still lake at different times, their circles intersecting as they expand and fade. The still lake now active with round waves looks very different and it only took 20 pebbles. What if ten people carried out two kind acts per day? It would transform their environment to one of caring and kindness where the mistreatment of others happened so rarely that no one would worry about being different or feeling isolated or making a mistake. If you are ready to throw a pebble or two, here are some ideas:

- Help around the house or classroom without being asked.
- Give a compliment.
- Say nice things about others when they are not around.
- Do not listen to or spread hateful comments or gossip.
- Pick up something someone dropped.
- Sit with someone who sits alone.
- Cheer someone on in gym class who rarely receives support.
- When someone says something negative about themselves, disagree.
- Give a card to someone.

Can you think of other kind actions you could try?

SELF-DIRECTED KIND ACTS

Many times we don't treat ourselves with as much kindness as we treat our friends and family. We can be hard on ourselves, blame ourselves, and be overly critical of our mistakes and weaknesses. These behaviors eat away at our self-esteem and multiply to hurt us on the inside and zap our radiance. While you increase your outward kind acts, increase your compassion for yourself. When you make a mistake, forgive yourself like you'd forgive a friend. Accept imperfections as a part of maturing and learning, for without them, no one would develop. Give yourself compliments and acknowledge your strengths while you use them to help others.

WHAT TO DO IF YOU ARE MISTREATED

If you find yourself on the receiving end of bullying behavior, do *not* keep it to yourself; privately inform an adult you can trust. Each and every person deserves respectful and kind treatment and if you receive disrespectful and unkind treatment it must stop. No one has the right to make you feel that way! Talking about what happened to an adult helps to heal the hurt and decreases feelings of isolation. You may find it helpful to talk to your school counselor, just like Eva spoke to Mrs. Spiagga. Your counselor may meet with you individually, or in a group. Don't hesitate to share your feelings; it is one of the many things you can do to care for yourself.

If for some reason the adult can't help or the mistreatment continues, inform another adult. Keep talking about it until it stops. In the meantime, try to be with another person in places where the mistreatment occurs (for example, the hallway or baseball field), preferably someone who might try out a SHIELD UP! strategy, or hang around by adults. If you feel comfortable, you can try to tell the person who is bullying you to stop, using the strong stance and voice outlined by Mrs. Spiagga, or you can use some humor to change the power balance. Your unexpected joke may throw off the person doing the bullying and give you time to walk away from the situation. Like the SHIELD UP! strategies, these strategies may not feel comfortable at first and are not easy. With some practice you may increase your comfort level with them and possibly be able to use one when you need it.

If the situation doesn't improve, or you feel distressed, talk to your parents about finding a licensed psychologist or mental health care provider to talk to. You don't have to go through this alone.

Whether you are observing mistreatment as a bystander, or you are the target of bullying behavior, or you find yourself acting as a bully, remember that you're not the only one facing these difficult situations and the feelings that go along with them. Don't forget that talking to adults about it can not only help you sort out your feelings but also helps stop the mistreatment of others. Whether or not you decide to SHIELD UP!, you don't need to handle it on your own. There are people all around that want to help, just ask.

ADDITIONAL RESOURCES

Listed below are websites that may be helpful if you are looking for more information about bullying, school concerns, health, and emotions.

KidsHealth: Feelings
www.kidshealth.org/kid/feeling
Resource for handling feelings and difficult situations at school, at home, or with friends. Learn about everything from plagiarism to test anxiety.

PBS Kids: It's My Life
www.pbskids.org/itsmylife
Play games, read stories, and watch videos on everything in life. It has information on topics from healthy eating to school concerns and coping with feelings.

Stopbullying.gov – Kids
www.stopbullying.gov/kids/
Learn all about bullying and its prevention through videos, stories, and games.

Pacer Center's Kids Against Bullying
www.pacerkidsagainstbullying.org
Play games, watch videos, take quizzes, or tell your story to help prevent bullying.

ABOUT THE AUTHOR

MARCELLA MARINO CRAVER, MSED, CAS, recently started a new career as a school counselor after nineteen years as a school psychologist in New Jersey and New York public schools. She is the author of *Learn to Study: A Comprehensive Guide to Academic Success* and *Chillax! How Ernie Learns to Chill Out, Relax, and Take Charge of His Anger. Chillax!* was awarded the Mom's Choice Gold Award for Juvenile Books—Self-Improvement and the Gold Moonbeam Children's Book Award for Comic Books/Graphic Novels. Her next book, *Joey Daring Caring and Curious: How a Mischief Maker Uncovers Unconditional Love,* is due out in fall 2014. Marcella lives with her wonderful husband, their two musically inclined teenagers, and a mischievous cat, who all fill her life with love, music, and laughter.

ABOUT THE ILLUSTRATOR

AMERIGO PINELLI lives in the heart of Naples, among narrow streets and churches. A long time ago, when he was a child, he met a pencil, and from that moment on he started to play, joke, fight, and make peace with it. He dreams of becoming a cartoon character...but some say that he already is. Since the birth of his daughter Chiara his life has been overfilled with color and overfilled with joy. He is over the moon!

You can find him chasing pigeons on the roof when the sun climbs on Vesuvio. Ask his wife, Giulia.

ABOUT MAGINATION PRESS

MAGINATION PRESS publishes self-help books for kids and the adults in their lives. Magination Press is an imprint of the American Psychological Association, the largest scientific and professional organization representing psychologists in the United States and the largest association of psychologists worldwide.